a minedition book

published by Penguin Young Readers Group

Text copyright © 1997 by Heinz Janisch
Illustrations copyright © 1997 by Lisbeth Zwerger
First minedition edition published in 2008
Original title: Die Arche Noah
First published in Switzerland in 1997 by Michael Neugebauer Verlag AG, ZH
English text adaption by Rosemary Lanning
Coproduction with Michael Neugebauer Publishing Ltd., Hong Kong.
Rights arranged with "minedition" Rights and Licensing AG, Zurich, Switzerland.
Published simultaneously in Canada.
Manufactured in China by Wide World Ltd.
Typesetting in Veljovic, by Jovica Veljovic
Color separation by Fotoreproduzioni Grafiche, Verona, Italy.

Library of Congress Cataloging-in-Publication Data available upon request.

ISBN 978-0-698-40082-5
10 9 8 7 6 5 4 3 2 1
First Impression

For more information please visit our website: www.minedition.com

ADAPTED BY HEINZ JANISCH

NOAH'S ARK

ILLUSTRATED BY LISBETH ZWERGER

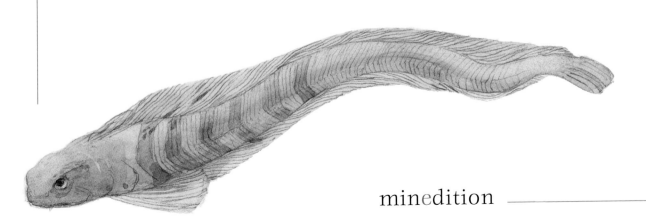

minedition

It came to pass in the days when giants strode the earth and were heroes among men, God saw that His people had grown wicked. They thought only of war and destruction.

And God was angry.

God said: "The people I created have become wicked, and do violent deeds. I will destroy them all, and cleanse the world of evil. Every living thing shall perish."

Among the people on earth there was one good man, whose name was Noah. Because he was righteous, Noah found favor in God's eyes, and God said to him: "All life on earth will end. I shall bring a flood, to cover the whole world. Everything that lives and breathes will die. But with you I will make a covenant. You shall survive. With you life will begin again after the flood.

"Go, and build an ark of cedar wood, big enough for yourself and your wife, your sons and your sons' wives. Take animals with you into the ark, two of each kind, one male and one female, so that they, also, may survive the flood.

"In seven days I will bring rain. The rain will fall for forty days and forty nights, and all life on earth will perish."

Noah built the ark as God had commanded. He cut planks of cedar wood, nailed them together, and coated them inside and out with pitch. He made the ark three stories high, with a wide doorway in the side.

Noah, his wife, his sons Shem, Ham, and Japheth made ready to go into the ark.

First they called the animals to the ark, two of each species that lived on earth, one male and one female of each kind. For God wished every species to live again after the flood.

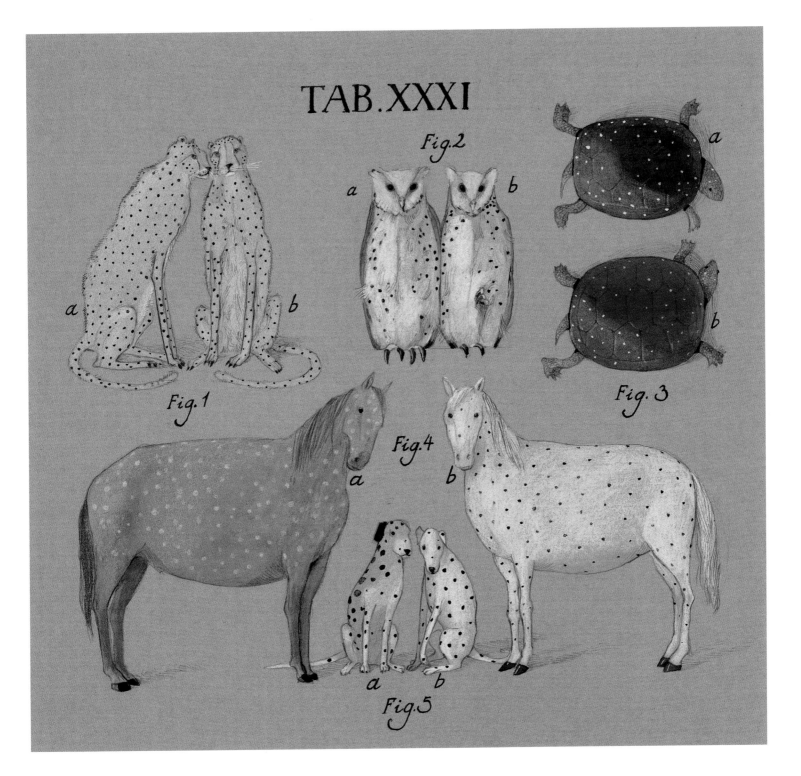

TAB.XXXI

Fig.1
a   *b*

Fig.2
a   *b*

Fig.3
a   *b*

Fig.4
a   *b*

Fig.5
a   *b*

Furred or feathered, from the ground, the treetops and the skies, from the mountains and the plains, from the fields and forests, the animals came.

Fig.1

a.

b.

T.127.

a.

b.

Fig.2

a.

b.

Fig.3

Fig.5

a.

b.

Fig.4

a.

b.

III.

From all corners of the earth the animals streamed into the ark, and there was room for all of them.

T. 573.

Fig. 1
a   b

Fig. 2
a

b

Fig. 3
a

b

When Noah, his wife, his sons, his sons' wives, and all the animals were safely in the ark, the rain began to fall. Night and day it rained without ceasing. Streams and rivers broke their banks. Ponds, lakes, and all the oceans overflowed.

The water rose and rose, lifting the ark higher and higher.
It flooded over everything, every village and town. No roof, tower, or mountain peak remained above the flood.
Water covered the whole earth. Everything on it was drowned.

Noah's ark floated alone across the waves.

Inside the ark, the animals were crowded close together, but they did not fight. Noah had plentiful stores of food for them and for his family.

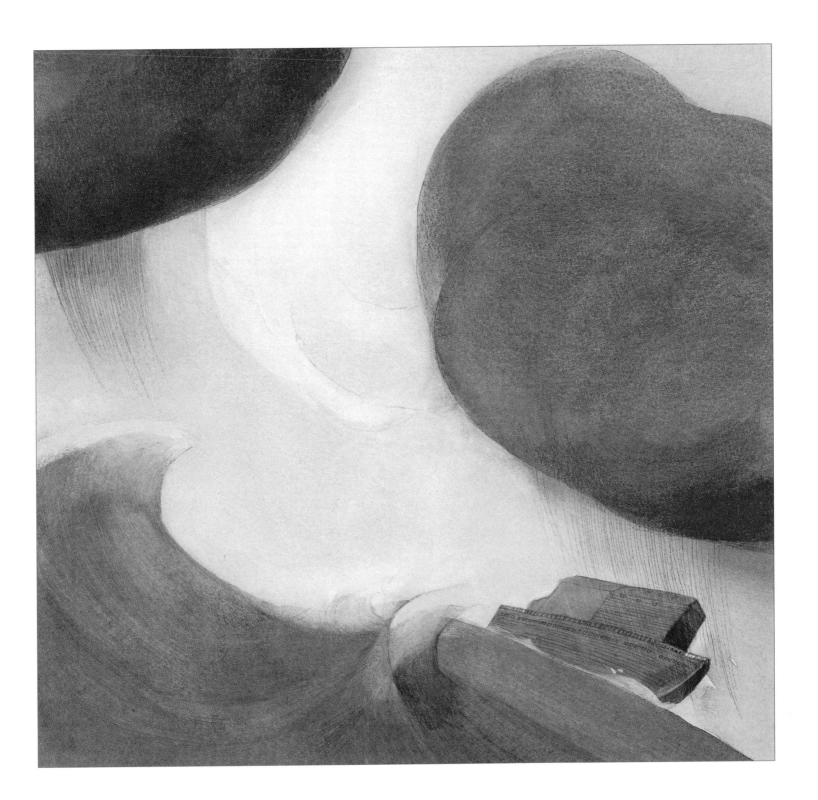

But they had many, many days to wait, floating above the flooded world. It seemed the rain would never stop.

Then, when it had rained for forty days and forty nights,
God remembered Noah and the ark, and the promise He had given.
The floodgates of heaven closed, the rain stopped, and slowly the
water began to drain away.
Mountain peaks appeared above the water.
The ark came to rest on one of them, Mount Ararat.

The animals in the ark were growing restless.

Noah sent out a raven. The raven flew to and fro across the endless water.

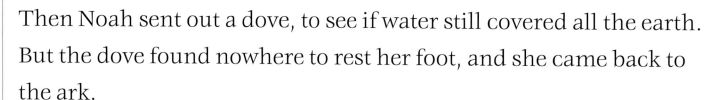

Then Noah sent out a dove, to see if water still covered all the earth. But the dove found nowhere to rest her foot, and she came back to the ark.

Noah waited seven days. Then he let the dove fly out again. In the evening she came back, with a fresh olive twig in her beak.

Noah waited another seven days; then he sent out the dove once more. This time she did not return.

So Noah opened a hatch and looked far out across the land, and he saw that the floodwater had drained away.

A drying wind blew across the land. The flood was gone, and it had washed the earth clean.

Noah opened the great door of the ark, and the animals streamed out. And Noah left the ark with his wife, his sons, and his sons' wives. God blessed them, and said: "Never again will I make a great flood to cover the whole earth. The seasons will return: seedtime and harvest, summer and winter.

"See, I have set my bow in the clouds. When clouds pass over the earth, the rainbow will be there among them. Let this be a sign that I will keep my promise to you and to future generations.

"Go forth now, be fruitful and multiply, and people the earth."

They looked up and saw a rainbow linking heaven and earth. And Noah went away from the ark, in hope and trust, and his offspring peopled the earth.

The following titles illustrated by Lisbeth Zwerger
are available from Penguin Young Readers Group:

THE LITTLE MERMAID · H.C. Andersen

THE NIGHT BEFORE CHRISTMAS · Clement Clarke Moore

THE BREMEN TOWN MUSICIANS · Brothers Grimm

HANS CHRISTIAN ANDERSEN'S FAIRY TALES · H.C. Andersen

LITTLE RED CAP · Brothers Grimm

HANSEL AND GRETEL · Brothers Grimm

ALICE IN WONDERLAND · Lewis Carroll